First published in 2021 by Scholastic Children's Books
Euston House. 24 Eversholt Street. London NW1 1DB
a division of Scholastic Ltd
www.scholastic.co.uk

London ~ New York ~ Toronto
Sydney ~ Auckland ~ Mexico City
New Delhi ~ Hong Kong

Text copyright © 2021 Michelle Robinson
Illustrations copyright © 2021 Tom Knight
PB ISBN 978 0702 30548 1

Printed in China
2 4 6 8 10 9 7 5 3 1

Papers used by Scholastic Children's Books are made from wood grown
in sustainable forests and other controlled sources.

Everyone was heading to the Kitchen Hall of Fame.
Fresh or canned or frozen, everybody felt the same.
Excited to be going where all dinners long to go:
to sit at the top table as the very . . .

"You'll miss the big announcement,"
Squirty Cream said. "Come on, mate!
We all deserve to be here, even Jelly on a plate."

Jelly on a plate! Jelly on a plate!
Wibble wobble! Wibble wobble!
Jelly on a plate!

Chicken nuggets, sausage rolls, falafel balls and more.

All piled on in and wondered who the golden crown was for.

Nervous Jelly tried to run . . .

WHO WILL WIN?

It's really not my thing. I'd rather put my jim-jams on and have a nice night in.

So Jelly found a quiet spot. He wasn't being rude.

"Come on, Jelly," Cake said. "You'll enjoy it, just you wait.
Make way, everybody! Here comes Jelly on a plate!"

Jelly on a plate! Jelly on a plate!
Wibble wobble! Wibble wobble!
Jelly on a plate!

The crowded hall fell silent as the
Biscuit took the stage.

Welcome, everybody, to a foodie golden age!
Tonight we crown a superstar. An all-time favourite food.
He's pretty shy and quiet, but he's still a total dude . . .

"I wibble in the middle and I wobble on the edge. I'm not at all nutritious like the healthy fruit and veg.

I'm silly and I'm frivolous. I've reached my use-by date!"

But Jelly's buddy Ice Cream said:

"Well, I still think you're great.
It's true you're shy and quiet, but you're also sweet and kind.
Come on, Jelly, sit with me. That is, if you don't mind . . . ?"

He felt a trifle better with a friend to sit beside.
Whoever won, he'd cheer them on with heartfelt foodie pride.
It did feel nice to be here and to share his fellows' fate.

We proudly pass the golden crown to . . .

Jelly sat there, wobbling.

"Did they really call my name?!"

"Yes, you wibble in the middle. Sure, you wobble on the edge.

You've not a lot in common with the healthy fruit and veg.
We know you think that's silly and it makes you feel quite small –
but we all feel like that sometimes.

JELLY REPRESENTS US ALL!"

Well, Jelly had a **wobble** as he stood there looking down.
But it felt quite good to **wobble** in a sparkly golden crown.

And there he wobbles on, the sweetest food you ever ate!
A much loved party favourite. Good old Jelly on a plate!

PARTY FOO